DISNEY · PIXAR
THE WORLD OF
Cars

The Big Race

Story retold by Kerry L. Bozza, Ed.D

Reader's
Digest
Children's Books®

Pleasantville, New York • Montréal, Québec • Bath, United Kingdom

*E*arly the next morning, McQueen needed gas before he set off for work. When
he found Sheriff at Doc's clinic, Doc shooed
him away. Upset, McQueen kicked an oilcan
with his tire. The can went flying into the air
and landed with a loud crash inside Doc's
garage. Even though there was a sign that said:
NO TRESPASSING on the garage's door,
McQueen wondered what he might have
broken and went inside.

Carefully, he went through the open door. The garage was a mess! And it was filled with junk. Off to one side, McQueen spied an object on Doc's desk. It was covered with dirt and dust and filled with tools. McQueen rolled over to it to take a closer look. McQueen could hardly believe his eyes! It was a Piston Cup! It was engraved: "HUDSON HORNET— CHAMPION, 1951."

McQueen was stunned. He turned and was shocked to see two more trophies lying on the floor nearby. He moved some junk out of the way to get a closer look. Next to them lay an old newspaper. Its headline proclaimed that

Doc, the Hudson Hornet, was the Champion for All Time.

Doc appeared in the doorway. He looked very angry.

"You're the Hudson Hornet!" exclaimed McQueen. "You still hold the record for the most wins in a single season!"

Doc wasn't happy that McQueen knew his secret. He moved behind McQueen and began to push him out the door. "Wait over at Flo's," he ordered.

"We've got to talk," begged McQueen. "You've got to show me your tricks, please!"

"I already tried that," said Doc as he slammed the garage door in McQueen's face.

Excited by what he had learned about Doc, McQueen zipped into town. "Oh, my gosh!" exclaimed McQueen when he saw Sheriff. "Did you know Doc is a famous race car?"

"Doc? Our Doc?" asked Sheriff.

"He's a real racing legend," continued McQueen. He explained that Doc was the Fabulous Hudson Hornet and had won three Piston Cups. He told everyone he met in town, but no one believed him.

"Kid's got a screw loose," one car said.

"Are you sick, buddy?" asked another.

Just then Sally arrived and gave McQueen a full tank of gas. Then she invited him to go for a drive. McQueen followed her up a tall

mountain, through a beautiful forest, past a
majestic waterfall, to a stop overlooking a huge
valley. "Wow!" cried McQueen. "What is this
place?"

Sally told him that Radiator Springs had
once been the most popular stop on the road.
Sally then explained that she used to be a
big-city attorney in California. But she had
been unhappy there. One day she had gone
driving and had broken down here in Radiator
Springs. "I fell in love," she admitted. And the

little town had become her new home.

In the distance McQueen could see the busy interstate. The cars were zooming past and didn't even notice the small town. Sally told him that before the interstate bypassed the town, Highway 66 had been the main road. "Back then," said Sally, "cars didn't drive on it to make great time. They drove on it to *have* a great time. Then the town got bypassed just to save ten minutes of driving."

When they got back into town, McQueen thanked Sally. "It's kind of nice to slow down every once in a while," he said.

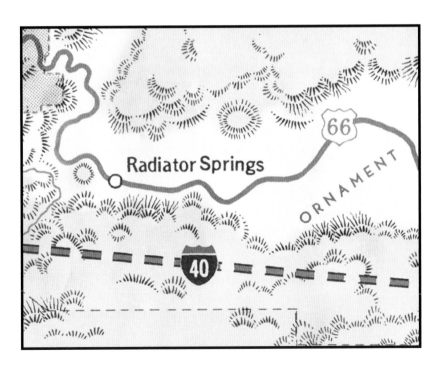

Suddenly, a stampede of escaped tractors stumbled through town. McQueen offered to help round them up. He followed one tractor out to a butte. When he got there, he saw Doc wearing his old racing tires. McQueen stopped and hid behind some brush. Then he watched in awe as Doc roared down the straightaway and around the track at top speed!

"Wow!" said McQueen, coming out of hiding. "You're amazing!"

Doc didn't know McQueen had been watching. He glared at the hotshot race car and, without a word, sped away. But McQueen wasn't going to let him go. He sped after Doc, who raced back to the garage.

"How did a car like you quit at the top of your game?" asked McQueen when he caught up to Doc.

"They quit on me!" snapped Doc. Doc explained that he had become injured in a car wreck. When he recovered, he was ready to race again, so he went back. But the racing world had forgotten all about him. It had replaced him with a hotshot rookie race car just like McQueen. "Just finish that road and get outta here," snapped Doc as he drove off, leaving McQueen standing by himself.

Once again, McQueen worked all night to finish the road. In the morning, it was done. When Sheriff told him he would give him a police escort so he could get to the race on time, McQueen said he couldn't leave yet. Before going, McQueen really wanted to help out his new friends. So McQueen became the best customer the town had seen in a long time! He got new whitewall tires, tried organic fuel, bought night-vision goggles and bumper stickers, and even got a new metallic paint job!

And that night, McQueen had a special surprise for Sally. At McQueen's signal, all the shopkeepers turned on their newly repaired neon lights. The town was lit up for the first time in years! Radiator Springs looked like a

new town. The cars cruised up and down the
newly paved Main Street. McQueen was so
happy! He looked over at Sally and wanted to
tell her how he felt.

Suddenly a bright spotlight shone down on
McQueen. Then a swarm of helicopters,
reporters, and photographers crowded around
him! They had been searching for him since
they'd discovered he was gone.

"We have found McQueen! We have found
McQueen!" announced a voice from a
helicopter that was circling above the crowd.

"You're here!" cried Mack as he drove
around the corner. "I'm sorry I lost you," he
told McQueen.

Soon Harv, McQueen's agent, and Mack convinced McQueen that it was time to go. He had to leave now in order to make the race on time. McQueen wasn't sure how to say good-bye. When he finally got to Sally, he didn't know what to say.

"Good luck in California. I hope you find what you are looking for," she said sadly. Then she turned and rolled through the crowd.

Soon the press closed in on McQueen. They pushed him back into his trailer. Moving quickly, Mack shut the trailer door and started to pull out of town. The press followed him, except for one reporter who stopped to thank Doc for tipping them off to McQueen's location. Sally overheard the reporter. Stunned, she gave Doc an angry look. "It was best for everyone," Doc tried to explain.

"Best for everyone? Or best for you?" demanded Sally. Then she and everyone else sadly headed home and turned out their lights. And just like that, the town was quiet again.

Soon, Mack and McQueen were at the racetrack. *Bang! Bang! Bang!* "Hey, Lightning, you ready?" asked Mack as he pounded on McQueen's trailer door.

"Yeah, yeah. I'm ready," said McQueen reluctantly. But McQueen wasn't really ready. Winning the biggest race of his life just didn't seem that important anymore.

"Hello, race fans, and welcome to what has become, quite simply, the biggest event in the history of racing—a three-way battle for the Piston Cup," said the announcer at the Los Angeles Speedway.

Two hundred thousand cars cheered as the race got underway. McQueen tried to battle with Chick and The King. But he just didn't have the desire to go fast. All he could do was

think about Sally and the other folks in Radiator Springs. Not paying attention to what he was doing, McQueen almost hit a wall! The crowd groaned!

"I don't know what's wrong with McQueen, but he's sure not driving like himself," the announcer commented.

Suddenly, a familiar voice came over McQueen's radio. "I didn't come all this way to

see you quit," said the voice. "I knew you needed a crew chief, but I didn't know it was this bad."

McQueen smiled. It was Doc! And he had pulled a pit crew together from Radiator Springs! The announcer and the crowd couldn't believe it. The famous Hudson Hornet was McQueen's crew chief!

Inspired, McQueen poured on the speed. Now he was going to win! Chick tried his best to run McQueen off the track. But McQueen used the backward driving he'd learned from

Mater to stay on. When Chick smacked hard up against him again, he used Doc's turn-right-to-go-left trick and took the lead. With help from his great pit crew, it looked as though McQueen was going to win!

Then, on the last lap, McQueen saw Chick ram into The King and send him rolling end over end. Approaching the finish line, McQueen looked up at the video screen and saw what had happened.

McQueen screeched to a stop. He couldn't let The King end his career like this! He had to help him!

McQueen let Chick zoom past. Then he put it in reverse and pushed The King across the finish line.

The whole stadium went crazy!

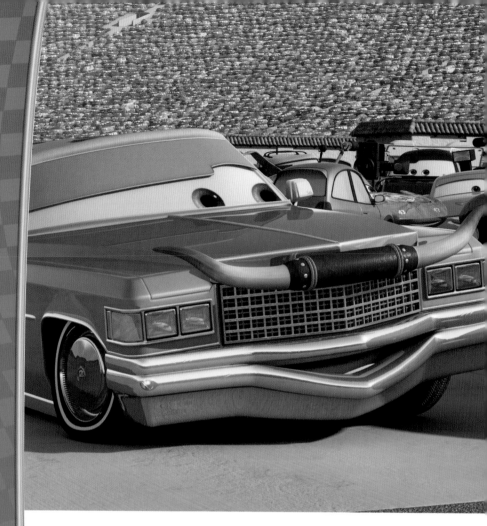

Tex, the owner of Dinoco, was so impressed with McQueen's generous behavior that he offered McQueen the Dinoco sponsorship.

"But I didn't win," said McQueen.

"Lightning, there's a whole lot more to racing than just winning," said Tex.

McQueen thanked Tex but decided that he was going to stay with Rust-eze, his original sponsor who had given him his first break.

However, he did ask Tex for one favor for his friend Mater.

Two days later, back in Radiator Springs, Sally was standing outside her motel when a familiar voice interrupted her thoughts. "There's a rumor floating around that some hotshot Piston Cup race car is setting up his big racing headquarters here."

It was McQueen! Sally smiled. She was happy he was back. And McQueen was happy to be back.

Right before he was about to tell Sally how he felt about her, he was interrupted by Mater, who was loudly cheering during his ride in a Dinoco helicopter.

McQueen looked up at his friend and laughed. The rookie had never been happier. He had found his home, good friends, and himself in Radiator Springs.